20

21

19

22 Your pony stops to eat grass. Miss two turns.

23

24

18

25

17 You urge your pony over a large jump — well done. Move on two squares.

26 Your friends cheer you on — move on a square.

16

27

15

28 A clear round! Gallop to the finish.

29

14

FINISH

13

WOULD you like to join in the fun of a pony show? Now you can — by playing our show jumping game. Each player will need a counter (a button will do). You will also need a dice.

Everyone places their counters on the 'START' square — then off you go, throwing the dice in turn.

The first person to reach the rosette is the winner.

Printed and Published by D. C. Thomson & Co., Ltd.,
Dundee and London

Dear Girls,
   "Twinkle" celebrates its 25th anniversary in 1993 — so this year's Twinkle Book is even more special than usual!
   As well as enjoying stories about all your favourite chums — you'll also find lots of super new stories to read — Moaning Minnie, The surprise present, "Dear Santa", and The sad snowman.
   There are lots of puzzles to do, too — and exciting games to play.
                    Have fun! Love, *Twinkle*

This book belongs to :
Name RIA
Address

Nurse Nancy

1 — It was almost Christmas and Nurse Nancy, who worked at the Dollies Hospital, was doing her Christmas shopping. Nancy *loved* Christmas, and choosing presents!

2 — Nancy was looking at some decorations when she spotted a special offer. "This tinsel would be just right for the tree in the ward," she smiled.

3 — Back at the hospital, Nancy was soon busy decorating the Christmas tree with the new tinsel — it *did* look pretty. "I've even got lots of tinsel left over," Nancy thought.

4 — Next, Nancy wrapped up the presents she had bought for her friends. The presents were so nice, Nancy knew everyone would like them.

5 — Then Nancy noticed that the patients looked a little sad. "Perhaps *they* would like a Christmas present too," Nancy thought. But the little nurse had no money left.

6 — Later, as Nancy put away the left-over tinsel, she suddenly thought of something she *could* do for the toys. "And it won't cost money," she smiled.

7 — Soon Nancy was busy with tinsel, baubles and glue. "I hope the toys like my idea," she thought. A teddy looked on with interest!

8 — Nancy had *made* Christmas presents for the toys from the spare decorations she had. The clever nurse now had lots of different things — bangles, ear-rings and hair bands!

9 — On Christmas Eve, the boys and girls arrived to take their toys home. "I've got a surprise for you," smiled Nancy. "Come inside and see."

10 — When the children saw their toys, they *were* thrilled. "They look lovely!" they cried. How jolly all the patients looked with their tinsel decorations.

11 — Some of the owners had presents for Nancy too — to thank her for looking after their toys. "Have a very Happy Christmas, everyone!" Nancy cried.

Moaning Minnie

MINNIE MOODIE was a naughty girl. Every time her mum asked her to do something, Minnie just whined and moaned.

"Oh, Minnie! What a mess!" sighed Mum one morning. "Help me clear up."

But Minnie wouldn't do a thing. She just sat at the table and mumped and moaned.

Unknown to Minnie, however, she was being watched by a tiny fairy at the window. It was the Bad Fairy.

"Goodee!" grinned the fairy. "She's just the sort of girl I'm looking for! Now I'll have some fun!"

3 — "I'm the Bad Fairy," answered the fairy, "and I just *love* people who make everyone else's life a misery by moaning all the time. I'll be happy here with you."

"You're not staying *here*!" snapped Minnie.

Minnie couldn't believe her eyes *or* her ears so she buried her head below her covers.

In the morning, she was wakened by the Bad Fairy tugging her toes.

"Ouch! Stop that!" yelled Minnie.

"That's the way to start the day — with a good moan," chortled the cheeky fairy.

2 — All day, the Bad Fairy watched as Minnie argued with her mum and stamped her feet.

"Tee-hee!" chuckled the fairy, keeping out of Minnie's sight.

"Wash your hands before tea, Minnie!" Mum called.

"They're not dirty," replied the little girl.

Later, Minnie screamed when Mum switched off the television set and put her to bed. She was *still* screaming when the Bad Fairy appeared at the foot of her bed.

"You're *definitely* the best moaner I've ever met, Minnie," laughed the fairy.

"Wh-who are you?" stammered Minnie.

4 — "I thought *you* were a bad dream," groaned Minnie.

"No, I'm *real*," smiled the Bad Fairy. "Now what else are you going to mump about? Come on, give me a good laugh."

When Minnie threatened to give her a slap, the fairy fell about laughing.

Just then, Mum shouted upstairs.

"Minnie! Are you awake? I want you to go to the shop for me!"

"I'm too tired!" Minnie called back.

"Ho! Ho! Ho!" laughed the Bad Fairy.

"Go away and leave me alone!" roared Minnie.

5 — But the Bad Fairy just danced gleefully before her.

"Get lost!" screeched Minnie.

"How can I leave when you're such fun, Minnie?" the fairy cackled.

As Minnie argued with the Bad Fairy, Mum's voice interrupted.

"Hurry up, Minnie!" she cried. "And wear your yellow dress today!"

"No! I *hate* it!" answered Minnie, rudely. "I'll wear what I like."

"You tell her," encouraged the Bad Fairy who was thoroughly enjoying herself — and annoying Minnie.

"Will you get out of here?" yelled Minnie. "What can I do to make you go?"

6 — "Why don't you try being nice for a change?" said a strange, new, tinkling voice.

Minnie looked up and, flying above her head, she saw *another* fairy.

This one looked *much* nicer than the other, though.

"Why don't *you* mind your own business?" the Bad Fairy told the new fairy. "Minnie and I are great friends. Push off!"

But the new fairy ignored her and whispered in Minnie's ear.

"I'm the Good Fairy," she said softly, "and the only way you'll get rid of the Bad Fairy is by being sweet and kind to people."

7 — Minnie was so fed up with the Bad Fairy that she decided to take the Good Fairy's advice. The little girl cleaned out her wardrobe then she made her bed and cleaned her room.

The Good Fairy fluttered around her shoulder making helpful suggestions and, after a while, Minnie found she was even beginning to enjoy herself!

The Bad Fairy, however, was having a tantrum!

"I don't believe it!" she howled. "She's *smiling*!"

The Bad Fairy wasn't the only one who couldn't believe the change in Minnie. Mum was delighted!

"Why, Minnie!" she gasped. "What a good girl!"

Next, Minnie said "sorry" to Mum for being so bad before.

When the Bad Fairy heard *that,* she could stand no more and she flew off through the window!

8 — "Hooray!" cheered Minnie. "She's gone! How can I thank you, Good Fairy?"

"I don't need thanks," answered the Good Fairy. "Just stay helpful."

"Don't worry," laughed Minnie. "No more moaning for me. *She* might come back!"

"Excellent," smiled the Good Fairy. "Then my work is done. I must go!"

"Can't you stay?" begged Minnie.

"No," sighed the fairy. "Besides, I think I'm going to be needed again. Look!"

And there was the Bad Fairy, merrily cackling on the shoulder of a child who was having a temper tantrum.

Pet puzzles

Lead the dog through the maze to find his kennel.

Rearrange the letters on the kennel to find the dog's name. The answer is given below.

ANEBRY

ANSWER — BARNEY

Can you match the pets with their favourite things?

CREAM

Find this cat's name by taking the first letter of each surrounding picture.

ANSWER — GINGER

Join the dots to find a pony.

Trace along the tangled wool to find which ball the kitten is playing with.

ANSWER — 3

Patch

1 — Paula Perkins has a cute kitten called Patch. He likes to join in whatever she does so he was *most* excited when she took him to her cousins' farm. They *did* enjoy meeting the hen's chicks.

2 — But the hen didn't like everyone crowding round — especially Patch! She flapped her wings at him as a warning.

4 — Paula's cousins took her to see the calves — but they were too *big* for Patch. Visiting the farm wasn't fun after all.

5 — "Cheer up, Patch," said Paula. "You'll enjoy yourself where we're going next . . ."

3 — Then the mother pig snorted angrily when Patch tried to make friends with her piglets.

6 — And he certainly did — for in the barn he met three tiny kittens! *They* wanted to play, too, and their mother didn't mind one little bit. At last Patch thought farm life was fun!

1 — Polly Penguin lives in Snowland. When her chum, Suki Seal, needed some help to clear out her attic, Polly offered. "What's that you've found?" asked Polly.

2 — It was a butterfly net. "Oh, let's go out so I can use it!" cried Suki excitedly. But the silly seal didn't realise that it was too cold for butterflies!

3 — She was determined to use the net somehow, so she thought she might catch a fish with it instead. "The fishing pond is frozen over!" grumbled Suki.

4 — "Huh! It's no use for anything!" sighed Suki, handing the net to Polly. "You take it. See if *you've* got any brilliant ideas!" With that, she waddled sadly off.

5 — Just then, Suki's mum came home from the shops. She slipped on the icy path and her shopping flew into the air.

6 — Quick as a flash, Polly caught it in the net! "Your net *did* catch something in the end, Suki!" laughed the penguin.

Cats, Cats, Cats!

THIN cats, trim cats,
   Cats that jump and play.
Fat cats, plump cats,
   That laze about all day.

Sleepy cats, dreamy cats,
   Cats that love to doze.
Bouncy cats, jumpy cats
   That keep you on your toes!

Stealthy cats, hunting cats,
   Cats that love to prowl.
Noisy cats, screechy cats
   That sit at night and yowl.

Naughty cats, wicked cats,
   Cats that love to tease.
Loving cats, happy cats
   That only want to please.

Silly Milly

Hospital

1 — Silly Milly is always in trouble. No matter what she does, it ends in a muddle. It was Christmas Eve, and Milly was off to visit her chum in hospital.

2 — "I've brought Cynthia grapes and holly because it's Christmas," smiled Milly, feeling very pleased with herself. "I'd hate to be in hospital at Christmas."

3 — Milly charged through the revolving doors at the hospital, but she caught her coat. There was a loud *ripping* sound, and Milly left most of her jacket behind.

4 — Racing down the corridor, Milly ran straight into a cleaner's trolley. "Ooomph! Sorry," she mumbled as she dropped the bunch of grapes on the floor.

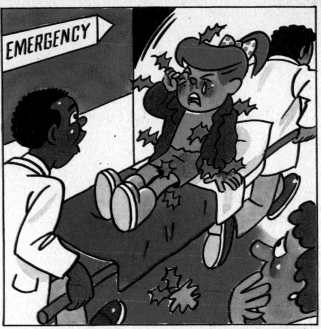

5 — Holding her nose, which was red and sore where the broom handle had hit it, Milly prepared to set off down the corridor. However, she slipped on the grapes.

6 — Milly landed on the holly and was in such a state that a stretcher was called for. "Boo! Hoo!" she howled as she was carried off with holly sticking everywhere.

7 — Christmas Day was bright and cheerful in the hospital. Santa Claus even arrived with nicely-wrapped presents.

8 — None of them was as well-wrapped as Milly, however, who was covered in bandages from head to toe. "What a super Christmas," said Mum. "It's certainly the first accident-free one *we've* had!"

Snow dreams

1 — When the wind blows from the north,
    Bringing flakes of white,
I lie snug in my little bed
    And close my eyes up tight.

2 — There's a tapping at the window,
    Jack Frost says, "Come and play."
He beckons with his icy hand
    And so we fly away.

3 — High above the roof tops,
    Where stars like lanterns glow,
Onward through the wintry night
    Towards the land of snow.

4 — Far beyond the Northern Lights,
Across a frozen sea,
To the Ice King's palace,
Just in time for tea.

5 — "Come in," he says, "please take a seat
And have some strawberry ice."
Although he looks quite frightening,
He's really very nice.

6 — Then back o'er the snowy waste,
Seated in a sleigh
Drawn by twenty reindeer,
We rush to break of day.

7 — Suddenly, I'm in my bed,
My cuddly's there with me.
I really think my tiny room's
The nicest place to be.

Cuddles and Co.

1 — Nadia loved animals and had lots of pets. One winter's day, it began to snow. Nadia *was* pleased. She loved snow — and so did her pets.

2 — Soon they were all having fun. Cuddles the dog and the rest of his friends liked playing with Nadia. The kind girl gave her dog a ride on her sledge.

3 — However, poor Nadia caught a cold and had to go indoors. "Now I won't be able to build a snowman," she sighed. Midge the cat felt sorry for the little girl.

4 — Midge told the other pets what she had heard Nadia say. Cuddles wondered what they could do to cheer her up. "I know!" he cried. "Come with me!"

5 — Cuddles had noticed that lots of snow had fallen on to the roof of the garden shed — and now it looked as if it was about to fall. "Quickly!" Cuddles barked.

6 — The pets were just in time. The snow fell from the roof, covering them completely. "Where did those snowmen come from?" Nadia gasped.

7 — In a flash, the pets shook themselves free from the snow. "It's *you*!" chuckled Nadia. "You *are* clever. What a lovely surprise you gave me!"

8 — Nadia brought her pets indoors to dry by the fire and to give them something to eat. "Having snow *pets* is much better than a snow*man*," she giggled.

The surprise present

Here's a special story . . . because you're the star! We've left blanks so you can fill in your name, and there are spaces to put in your best friend's name. There's also a blank where you can stick down your own photograph, and really make the story your own. Have fun!

IT was almost Christmas. .RIA.... was very excited. She'd written her letter to Santa, and asked him for a very special present — a .... hoped she would get it.

But now .RIA.... had her own Christmas shopping to do. So she emptied all her savings from her piggy bank, and phoned her best friend, .Cheryl..

"Would you like to come shopping with me, .Yes...?" .RIA... asked. "You can help me choose my Christmas presents."

"That would be great fun!" .Cheryl. replied. "I'll come round right now."

So, soon, the two friends were in a large department store in the middle of town.

The store was decorated with all sorts of pretty decorations. .RIA.... and *Cheryl* were quite excited to see the tinsel, baubles and trees.

.they. had lots of presents to buy, but the shop was filled with so many nice things, that before long .RIA... had bought nearly all the presents she needed.

"I've bought something for Mummy, Daddy, and .Brother .She... smiled. "Now all I need is something for Gran."

But although .RIA... thought as hard as she could, she couldn't think *what* to buy.

"What about a nice scarf?" suggested her friend.

"Gran's got lots of scarves," .She... sighed.

2 — "Chocolates?" asked ...Cheryl...

"Mummy's giving her some," ...Ria... replied.

....Ria... decided to go home and ask her mummy if she knew what she could buy.

Mummy couldn't think of anything either.

"Why don't you phone Gran to ask her?" Mummy suggested.

.... did just that. Gran *was* pleased to hear from her grand-daughter. .... and her family lived a little way off, so Gran didn't see them very often.

"As long as I see you all, I don't need a present," Gran said. "Just you bring yourself on Christmas Day, and I'll be happy."

.... promised she would . . . but she *still* wanted to buy her gran something.

Then .... knew just what she could give her gran.

The little girl hurried to a nearby gift shop and made a purchase.

You can stick down a photograph of yourself or your family in this space.

3 — Then, back home, ... searched through the drawer where Mummy kept old bills, writing paper and photographs. .... took something from the drawer.

On Christmas Day, ... was up bright and early to open her presents.

Then the family set off to visit Gran.

Gran was delighted to see everyone, and was even more pleased when .... handed her a present.

And when Gran opened her present, she was thrilled! It was a lovely photo frame, and inside it was a picture of .... and her family.

"Now we'll be with you all the time, Gran," .... smiled.

Gran carefully put the photograph on her mantelpiece.

"It's my most favourite present of all," Gran said, and she gave her grand-daughter a hug.

FIONA had never been skiing and she wondered what it would be like.

So we decided to take her to Glenshee in Scotland to find out.

2 He-e-lp! Fiona landed on the snow. "Mmm! This is tricky," she cried. "My skis are tangled and I can't get up!"

3 Time for a lesson. Alan, a ski instructor gave Fiona a little help. Here they are trying the snowplough position.

1 Once Fiona was kitted out with ski equipment, she put on her skis. Then it was time to head for the nursery slopes.

SKIIN

6 Fiona managed to ski down the nursery slope.

7

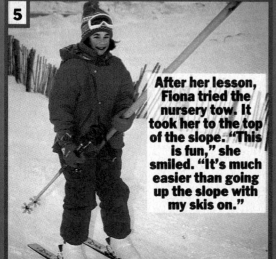

5 After her lesson, Fiona tried the nursery tow. It took her to the top of the slope. "This is fun," she smiled. "It's much easier than going up the slope with my skis on."

Next, Alan showed Fiona the racing position.

FUN

"I can ski now!" smiled Fiona. "I've had a super time today. Thank you, Twinkle."

8 After an hour or two on the nursery slopes, Fiona was doing really well. Now she was able to race down the slopes.

She almost made it to the bottom without . . . falling! Oops! Better luck next time. "I'm glad this snow's soft," giggled Fiona.

What a show off!

WEE Benny's sweet, but seldom neat,
    He's full of fun and joy.
He's grubby, friendly, naughty, cute,
    Like any little boy. He's . . .

My Baby Brother

BEN loves to go out shopping
    Along with Mum and me.
At first, it's to the baker man,
    To buy some buns for tea.

The shoe shop next, for Benny needs
    New shoes to wear, Mum said.
He chose a really jazzy pair,
    With laces of bright red.

Then at the fruit shop, cheeky Ben
    Said, "Cherries would be nice!"
Mum bought some in a little bag —
    They vanished in a trice!

The fishmonger's a jolly man.
    He gave young Ben a wink.
"Know what you'll have for tea tonight?
    It's fish and chips, I think!"

The butcher's shop has little trays
    Of meat, for all to see.
Ben tugged at Mummy's sleeve, and said,
    "Please, sausages for me!"

The chemist shop smells beautiful,
    With perfume everywhere.
Mum bought some soap. She smiled at Ben.
    "To wash behind each ear!"

At the Pets' Parlour, next, we found
    Some food for goldfish Fred.
"I wish I had that puppy dog!"
    My funny brother said.

At last, our shopping was all done.
    Kind Mummy took us to
A cafe, for a big ice cream,
    And guess who gobbled *two*?

Elfie

Elfie is a tiny elf who secretly lives in Mary's doll's house. When he makes things happen, Mary thinks there's magic at work! Poochie, Mary's dog, is Elfie's friend. It was nearly Christmas.

1 — "I've no present to give Mary," the little elf wailed sadly as he watched Mary help put up the decorations. "Don't worry," Poochie told him. "I'm sure you'll think of something."

2 — Mary had a problem. "I *do* like decorating the Christmas tree," she sighed, "but there's always *such* a mess to clear up afterwards. I don't enjoy *that*."

3 — So, instead of tidying the room, Mary went out to play, while *Elfie* gathered up the left-over pieces of glitter and fir tree. "Now I know what I can give Mary," he chuckled.

— Elfie then went to Mary's mummy's ewing basket and borrowed a thimble. "I can se these beads from her broken necklace, oo," the elf smiled. His plan was taking shape!

5 — He stood a twig from the fir tree in the upturned thimble and then fixed glitter and some of the beads on it. It looked just like a miniature Christmas tree!

6 — When Mary returned, she was *amazed* to find the tiny tree in her doll's house. "The magic has given me a Christmas present," she gasped. "Not the magic — *me*," smiled Elfie. "But that's *our* secret, Poochie!"

The sad snowman

1 — Sarah was building a snowman. She worked very hard and finally, the snowman was finished. "I'll call you Freddie," she decided.

2 — But Freddie looked sad. "I wonder what's wrong?" Sarah puzzled. "Perhaps he's cold." The little girl hurried indoors to fetch him a scarf to wear.

3 — Sarah tied the scarf round the snowman's neck. "Perhaps *that* will make him smile," she thought. But Freddie *still* looked glum as he stood in the garden.

4 — Next Sarah gave Freddie smart buttons to wear and a jolly hat for his head. But the snowman wouldn't smile at all. Sarah didn't know *what* to do.

5 — A little later, Sarah's schoolmates came round to play and soon they were having fun. "It's nice to have people to play with," Sarah decided.

6 — When her chums had gone, Sarah noticed that Freddie had two icy tears running down his cheek. It was then that she realised what was wrong — Freddie was lonely!

7 — So Sarah set to work to make a second snowman right next to Freddie. "Now you have a friend," she told him. It was growing dark and soon Mummy called Sarah inside for tea.

8 — Next morning, Sarah went to see Freddie — and to her delight, he was *smiling*. Sarah decided to tell all her friends to always build *two* snowmen!

Witch Winkle

Wendy Wilson has a very unusual friend — a witch called Winkle. She is three hundred years old and lives in Wendy's attic. Winkle has a magic wand and broomstick.

1 — One night, Wendy's mum and dad were going to a ball. "I wish I had a new dress," sighed Mum, looking in the mirror. "That one's not very fashionable," agreed Wendy.

2 — But there was worse to come. "The car won't start," groaned Dad, "and it's too late to get a taxi." Poor mum was nearly in tears. "What can we do?" she cried.

3 — Wendy knew what to do. She ran up to the attic and shook Winkle. "Wake up, Winkle!" she called. "We need your help to get Mum and Dad to the ball." "Go away," grumbled Winkle, sleepily.

4 — But when Wendy explained, Winkle, half-asleep, waved her wand. *Whoosh!* In a flurry of stars, Mum got her new dress — but she looked like someone out of a fairy tale!

5 — "Where's my car?" roared Dad. It had vanished, and in its place was a coach and four white horses. "We'll *never* get to the ball in time in *that*!" cried Dad.

6 — Suddenly, a cry came from the children next door. "What have you done with our rabbits?" they asked. "And where's my prize pumpkin?" asked another neighbour.

7 — "What *have* you done, Winkle?" asked Wendy, crossly. "Sorry, I was so sleepy I did a 'Cinderella' spell and got it wrong," mumbled the silly witch. "You'd better sort it out then," scolded Wendy.

8 — "Oh, all right," sighed Winkle huffily, and once again, she waved her wand. The horses changed back to rabbits, the coachman became a pumpkin and the coach turned back to Dad's car.

9 — The neighbours were happy to help when Wendy explained. "I can lend you a dress," offered the children's mum. "And you can borrow my car," said the man.

10 — Quick as a flash, Mum changed into the other dress and soon she was on her way to the ball with Dad. "Have a nice time!" cried everyone as they waved them off.

11 — Wendy chuckled when she thought of the commotion Winkle's spell had caused. "You're a silly old witch sometimes, Winkle, but your spells always come right in the end," she laughed.

Bobbie

2 — "I think everyone's decided to stay indoors today," Mummy smiled.

Bobbie didn't mind because she liked to stay inside and read.

But later her friend, Carly, phoned.

"I've got a cold and have to stay in bed," Carly sighed. "I've played with *all* my games, and I'm bored. Please come and visit me."

Bobbie didn't know *what* to do! She wanted to visit her friend, but how would she get through the snow?

"Eskimos wouldn't let a little snow bother them," Bobbie smiled, and then she had a plan!

The little girl put on her warmest coat with its fur-trimmed hood, then looked out her sledge from the garden shed.

Bobbie loves reading! And when she's reading a particularly good story, she sometimes just has to join in!

ONE day, Bobbie was reading a story all about Eskimos who lived in Alaska, where there was always snow.

"I don't think I'd like to live somewhere it snowed all the time," thought Bobbie.

"But there's no chance of that," she smiled. "We haven't had any snow this winter."

However, when Bobbie went to bed that night, it *did* snow.

The snow lay deep on the ground. Bobbie looked out of her window, and noticed that there were hardly any people or cars around.

3 — Next, she selected some of her favourite games, which she tied to the sledge. Finally she strapped the tennis rackets to her feet to use as *snow* shoes!

"Just like the Eskimos did in my book!" Bobbie chuckled.

Pulling her sledge behind her, Bobbie walked through the snow easily, thanks to her special shoes, and in no time she was at her friend's house.

Carly *was* pleased to see her!

The two girls had a lovely time playing with Bobbie's games, and Carly's mum made them a special Eskimo tea — fish fingers, with ice cream to follow!

They *did* have fun!

On Christmas Eve...

WHEN I walked out on Christmas Eve,
   I saw the snowflakes falling.
A robin on the holly tree
   Was calling, calling, calling.

The twinkly stars were cold as ice,
   The sleigh bells softly ringing,
And carollers along the lane
   Were singing, singing, singing.

I thought, "Across the frosty sky
   The reindeer will be prancing.
As happy children everywhere
   Are dancing, dancing, dancing!"

So home I raced, fast as could be,
   On mince pies to be dining . . .
While lights upon our Christmas tree
   Were shining, shining, shining.

Puzzle time

Can you find six differences between these two pictures?

Which two plants are exactly the same?

Rearrange the letters to find the names of four things found in a lounge.
ANSWERS — RUG, PICTURE, SETTEE, LAMP.

Join the dots to find a plant.

You can colour this picture using your paints or crayons.

Ted and Zed

from Outer Space

1 — ONE afternoon, Ted and Zed met Susie. "I'm going to a Christmas party," she smiled. "Would you like to come along?" "Oh, yes!" they laughed.

2 — At the party, Ted had great fun playing games with the other children. "It'll soon be time for tea," Susie told Zed, "and then Santa Claus arrives with presents." "That sounds good," smiled Zed. "I can't wait!"

3 — After tea, the children waited patiently for Santa Claus to arrive. "I wonder what's happened to Santa?" sighed Susie. "He's *never* late!" "We could go and look for him," suggested Zed. "Oh, that's a good idea!" said Ted. And off they went.

4 — In no time, Ted and Zed found Santa Claus. "My reindeer have caught flu and they can't pull my sleigh," he explained. But the two chums had a plan.

5 — Soon, Santa arrived at the party in Ted and Zed's *space* car. Everyone clapped and cheered.

6 — "I may need your help on Christmas Eve," Santa chuckled. "If my reindeer still have flu!"

The toy circus

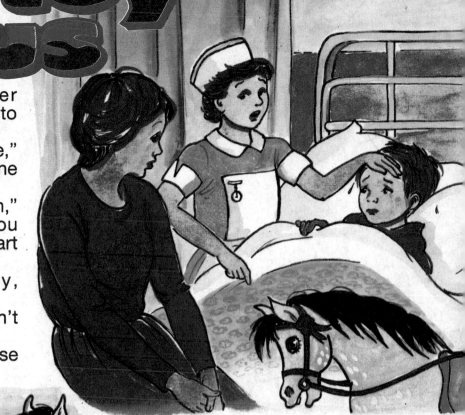

POOR Christine Carter wasn't well and had to spend some time in hospital.

"I don't want to stay here," she cried. "I want to go to the circus."

"You aren't well enough," sighed Mummy. "And you won't get strong until you start to eat again."

"But I'm not hungry, Mummy," sighed Chris.

"You must eat or you won't get better," said the nurse.

Robin the rocking horse heard every word.

2 — That night, when everyone was asleep, Robin rocked slowly across to the toybox.

"Waken up!" he whispered.

"What's the matter, Robin?" asked Teddy Bear.

"We must help Chris," said Robin. "Waken the others."

Teddy ducked back into the toybox and shook the others awake. Elephant, Monkey, Toy Soldier and the dolls climbed out, yawning. When everybody was ready, Robin began.

"Chris is very disappointed at missing the circus and she won't eat," he told them. "And if she doesn't eat, she won't get better."

"What can *we* do, Robin?" asked Elephant.

3 — "I don't know," said Robin. The toys sat and thought. Then Clown jumped up. "Got it!" he said. "We'll have a circus right here!"

4 — "That's a great idea, Clown," said Monkey. "I'll be the acrobat." And he swung round the leg of a chair just to show what he could do.

5 — "I'll be the circus horse," said Robin. "And Ballerina Doll can balance on my back."

Soon, all the toys had something to do.

"Right!" said Teddy, later. "Toy Soldier, get ready to waken Chris."

Toy Soldier stood on the bed and Teddy Bear gave the signal. When Toy Soldier beat his drum, Chris opened her eyes.

"The circus has come to town!" announced Toy Soldier.

Chris sat up and stared at the circus on the floor. The dancing dolls led the way, followed by the juggling clown and Robin with Ballerina Doll. Then Clown did tricks.

6 — Next, Monkey surprised Chris by swinging round the bedhead and leaping about.

"Ooh! This is a wonderful circus," said Chris.

When Chris grew tired, the toys gathered for the final parade.

"Goodnight. Get well soon," they chorused.

"Goodnight," replied Chris. "That was the best circus in the world!"

When Chris wakened next morning, her mum and the nurse were beside her bed.

"Hello, Mum. I was at the circus last night," smiled the little girl.

"You must have been dreaming," laughed Mum.

"I wasn't," protested Chris. "When's breakfast? I'm hungry."

"Her dream has helped her get better," said the nurse, pleased.

Robin and his friends were very happy, too.

Fairy Fay

1 — It was almost Christmas and the streets of Fairytown were busy with shoppers. "I love this time of year, don't you?" Fairy Fay asked her friend, Andy Imp.

2 — Fay still had some presents to buy. "I think I'll have to come into town again tomorrow," she said. "Me too," Andy agreed. "But shopping's fun, isn't it?"

3 — When Fay looked out of her window the following morning, she *did* get a surprise! It had been snowing and now the snow lay deep on the ground.

4 — Fay's warm cloak made her journey hard work. On the way, she stopped to chat to Mrs Berry. "I don't think I'll manage to go to town today," the lady sighed.

5 — Fay hurried to Nobby Gnome's house and told him to get out his train from its shed. "My train?" he cried. "But I don't run my train during the winter!"

6 — Nobby did as Fay asked, and soon the Fairyland Express was chugging along its track. "All aboard!" cried Fay. "We're going shopping, everyone!" They *were* puzzled!

7 — Even though the snow made it difficult to walk, the train could still run! "Next stop Fairytown!" cried Nobby to the fairy folk.

8 — "We'll be able to finish our shopping after all!" chuckled Andy Imp. And everyone in Fairyland had a very Happy Christmas!

Puzzle and Play time

Can you lead the children through the maze to reach their house?

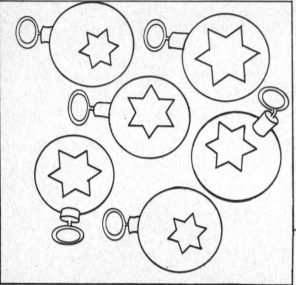

Which two baubles are exactly the same?

A I
F N
O

Rearrange the letters above to find the fairy's name. The answer is given below.

ANSWER — FIONA

These children are decorating their Christmas tree. Count the stars in the picture then colour it.

ANSWER — 9 STARS

Sam

SHONA MACGREGOR has a clever sheepdog called Sam. They live on a farm in the Scottish Highlands.

One afternoon, Shona sat at the kitchen table trying to do her homework. She had been asked to draw a winter scene for an art class competition, but she wasn't getting on very well.

"I can't think of a good idea at all," she sighed wearily. "I'd like to draw something *unusual*."

Try as she might, though, nothing came to mind and, when Sam suddenly burst into the room, Shona rounded on him angrily.

"Go away, Sam," she cried. "How can I concentrate when you keep barking at me?"

But Sam wouldn't give up and when finally he tugged at her sleeve, Shona realised that the dog was trying to tell her something.

"I'm sorry I snapped at you, Sam," Shona apologised. "I was just being a crosspatch. Show me what you're wanting."

And as Shona stood up, Sam turned and raced outside.

2 — Shona followed quickly behind Sam, but she *was* puzzled when they reached the garden. Nothing seemed to be amiss.

Then Shona noticed that the bird-table had fallen over.

"Is *that* all?" she asked. "You didn't have to disturb me because of *that*."

3 — Sam trotted over to the coconut that was lying beside the table, however, and began pawing the ground.

When Shona went closer to investigate, she *did* get a surprise. Faint noises came from underneath the shell!

"There's something inside!" the little girl gasped, and, sure enough, when she lifted the shell, out flew a robin!

"He must have been feeding from the coconut when the table blew over and trapped him. It's a good job Sam heard the noise!" Shona smiled. "Well done, Sam."

But Shona still had her homework to do and so she reluctantly turned back inside.

4 — Before she started sketching again, Shona decided to have a break and watch her favourite TV pop programme.

"Perhaps it will give me some inspiration," she thought, "because I can't think of *anything* to draw."

No sooner had she settled comfortably in front of the television screen, however, than Sam walked between it and Shona and sat down.

"Sam!" cried Shona crossly. "I can't see a thing now. Move over."

But the sheepdog only gave a little whimper and looked over towards the windowsill.

Shona's eyes then followed . . . and there, sitting peering in the window, was the robin she had rescued.

"So you've come back," she smiled. "Is it to say 'thank you', or are you trying to tell me you're hungry?"

Shona went to fetch some birdseed.

5 — She scattered some seed on the ledge and Sam watched closely as the robin pecked happily at it.

"Why, that would be the perfect winter picture!" Shona suddenly realised, and rushed off to fetch her sketching pad and pencil.

The robin was quite unafraid as Sam pressed his nose against the glass and Shona quickly sketched the scene.

"Best of all, *you'll* be in the picture, too, Sam," she chuckled.

Shona was soon able to paint the drawing and hand it in at school.

All the pictures were put on the art class wall — and when the results of the competition were read out, Shona was awarded first prize.

She asked if Sam could be with her when she was given the prize.

"After all," explained Shona, "if Sam hadn't rescued the robin and then given me the idea of what to draw, I wouldn't have won the prize in the first place!"

Christmas puzzles

FAR, far away in snowy lands
Where reindeer sport and play,
You'll find a dear, old, jolly man,
Who owns a magic sleigh.

Which reindeer is the odd one out?

Do you know
his name?
The answer
is given below.

ANSWER — RUDOLPH the red nosed reindeer.

He has a workshop where his elves
Make lots of super toys.
They know exactly what will please
All little girls and boys.

Can you find 10 things
beginning with the letter
"B" in this picture?
The answers are
given below.

ANSWERS —
BANANA, BALL, BAT, BIKE,
BEAR, BASKET, BALLOON,
BOOKS, BOX, BIRD.

On Christmas Eve, the jolly man
Flies off into the night
Upon his toy-filled, magic sleigh.
It is a splendid sight!

Join the dots to find a sleigh.
Then find 6 Christmas crackers
hidden on these two pages.

The dear, old man delivers toys
To every girl and boy.
He wants to make their Christmas Day
So full of fun and joy.

for Santa

Lead Santa through the maze to reach Sally's bedroom.

You can colour
this picture.

Now, who is this old, jolly man
Who's never, ever cross?
"Of course!" you shout. "We know him well,
His name is Santa Claus!"

How many elves are in this picture?
The answer is given below.

ANSWER — 12

Blow, wind, blow!

THE wind woke up one day feeling very mischievous.

"I think I'll have fun," he chuckled, and he puffed his cheeks, ready to blow.

Passing a farm, he saw the farmer's wife hanging out her washing.

"The wind's a bit strong today," she muttered.

Just then, the wind huffed and puffed and blew the washing away.

2 — "Ho, ho, ho!" he laughed as a runaway shirt draped itself around Daisy Cow. "That suits you, Daisy!"

Next, a handkerchief landed on Penny Pig's head like a sun bonnet.

"Ha, ha, ha!" chortled the wind. "What fun!"

3 — He hurried over to the other side of the hill where he knew the children would be heading for school.

"I'll help them along," he smiled, and he gave an extra-strong puff.

The children chuckled as Kirsty's hat flew off and Hayley's books were whisked from her arms. The wind was blowing so strongly that it was a struggle to stop.

"Whee! My feet are hardly touching the ground!" cried Jamie.

4 — In the village street, Mr Pastry the baker was carrying pies to his van when the wind decided to tug at his hat.

The naughty wind held his sides laughing as Mr Pastry, trying to hold on to his hat, tipped his tray of pies. As they tumbled to the ground, all the neighbourhood dogs rushed to help clear up — *and* have a lovely dinner!

"How can I make *more* mischief?" the wind wondered.

5 — Just then, it began to rain.

"I'll play in the park before it gets too wet," gasped the wind.

And he ran through the park, chasing leaves, until he spotted his favourite plaything — an umbrella!

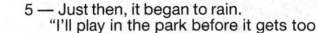

With a mighty blow, he snatched it from an old lady's hand and sent it soaring through the air.

6 — When the umbrella landed upside-down in the duck pond, some ducks thought it was a boat and they hopped in.

"How lovely!" exclaimed the umbrella's owner as the ducks floated in to the river bank in their umbrella boat.

She took a photograph.

"This is *sure* to win the Camera Club competition," she smiled. "Thank you, Mr Wind!"

Now the naughty wind felt quite humble. No one had ever thanked him before for his pranks and he went off home, quite happily, to rest.

It's panto time!

Junior Showtime
presents
The
Wizard of Oz
starring
LYNN LOW
as
Dorothy

It's pantomime time again and when we saw that The Wizard of Oz was being staged nearby, the Twinkle team just *had* to go along — especially when the star of the show is a "Twinkle" reader!

We were lucky enough to meet our little star, Lynn Low, on her way to the dress rehearsal. "Hi!" said Lynn. "Come in and meet the rest of the company."

"They're looking quite smart just now," laughed Lynn, "because they're wearing their Junior Showtime costumes. That's Margaret, our producer, trying to knock them into shape."

Lynn told us that when she joined the company, she had to learn to dance and sing. "Margaret teaches us just about everything," she said. We asked Lynn how it felt to be a 'star'. "Really *busy*," she grinned. "I couldn't believe it to begin with and I haven't had time to think about it since.

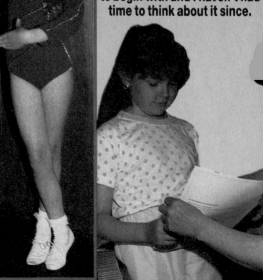